This book is given to my "Little One."

Name: _____

Date: _____

From: _____

WinePress Publishing (PO Box 428, Enumclaw, WA 98022) functions only as book publisher. As such, the ultimate design, content, editorial accuracy, and views expressed or implied in this work are those of the author.

Unless otherwise noted, all Scriptures are taken from the Holy Bible, New International Version, Copyright © 1973, 1978, 1984 by the International Bible Society. Used by permission of Zondervan Publishing House. The "NIV" and "New International Version" trademarks are registered in the United States Patent and Trademark Office by International Bible Society.

ISBN 1-57921-849-0
Library of Congress Catalog Card Number: 2005909812

Printed in Korea

Little One

Ernest E. Finklea

Illustrated by Dane Snyder

This book is dedicated to my beloved wife, Melanie,
and to my precious grandchildren:
Hannah Katherine
Josiah David
Andrew Stephen
Abigail Elizabeth
Allison Jennifer-Lynn
Joseph Benjamin

It is my prayer that each of you will always be a "Little One."
~Poppe

Thank you, Ernest, for blessing me with the opportunity
to take part in sharing your extraordinary tale.
~Dane

Dear Reader,

Before you turn the pages of this book
And bring to life this tale of hope and trust,
Affix your gaze upon that little child
Who is content to rest within your care,
And marvel at the handiwork of God.

Within that precious countenance and form,
Lies steadfast strength of heart and hand divine.
For Christ, our Lord, has chosen innocence
To hold love's banner firm and show the way
To His profound embrace through simple faith.

It is an awesome thing to realize;
We stand beneath the shadow of a child
Whose tender mind walks not in intellect,
Yet holds the truth of who we ought to be.
Oh reader, take that hand and hold it tight!

For the Lord loves the just
and will not forsake his
faithful ones. They will be
protected forever...
Psalm 37:28

Little One

There was a time long ago when the animals of the earth listened to the voice of God. And so it was that one day a community of mice gathered together. In the language of animals, they were called Small Eyes of the Little Feet.

He who was the oldest stepped forward. "The Maker of Life," he said, "has need of one of you."

He who was the wisest held his head up high.

He who was the strongest breathed deeply.

He who was the bravest stepped forward a little.

Each one thought to himself, "I will help the Maker of Life."

"One of you," continued he who was the oldest, "must journey through the Land of the Deep Grass and cross the Great Mountain that Touches the Sky.

You must then make your way through the Great Forest and cross the Water of the Deep Bottom until you reach the Land of the Tamer of Beasts. The Maker of Life will guide you."

He who was the wisest lowered his head. He thought to himself, "Should I trust the Maker of Life? I have never seen a Tamer of Beasts. Perhaps he is not real."

He who was the strongest found his breath to be short. He thought to himself, "It is too far for me to go. I would become weak and surely die."

He who was the bravest stepped back a little. He thought to himself, "I am so very small. What if I should meet a great beast along the way?"

"Now," said he who was the oldest. "Who will help the Maker of Life?"

No one answered. And then, she who was the youngest stepped forward. She was called Little One because she was the smallest of her kind.

"I will go," she said.

"It is a very long journey," said he who was the oldest. "Are you not afraid?"

"No," she said. "If the Maker of Life will show me the way, I have nothing to fear."

He who was the oldest looked into her trusting eyes. "Then come," he said, "and I will show you where your journey must begin." He led her to the place where the Land of the Deep Grass began and watched her as she slowly disappeared into the tall grass.

Consider it pure
joy...whenever you face
trials of many kinds,
because you know that the
testing of your faith
develops perseverance.
James 1:2

Little One was almost hidden as she made her way through the Land of the Deep Grass. Suddenly she stopped. She could see something slowly crawling toward her.

All at once, a large head appeared. It was Swallower of Life! Little One knew that Swallower of Life ate the Small Eyes of the Little Feet, but she did not run away.

"Well now," he said, "going somewhere?" And he moved his head a little closer.

"The Maker of Life is sending me on a journey to the Land of the Tamer of Beasts," she said.

Swallower of Life thought for a moment. "How can you know where you are going," he asked, "when you cannot see beyond the deep grass?"

Little One answered, "I do not need to see what is beyond me if the Maker of Life is guiding the steps I take."

Swallower of Life looked into her trusting eyes. "I will help the Maker of Life," he said. "I will take you through the Land of the Deep Grass."

Little One climbed upon his back, and carefully he slithered back and forth until the tall grass was behind them. Before her, she could see the Great Mountain that Touches the Sky. As she slid off his back, she thanked him for his kindness and went on her way.

He will cover you with his feathers, and under his wings you will find refuge; his faithfulness will be your shield and rampart.

Psalm 91:4

Little One stood before the Great Mountain that Touches the Sky. "I wonder," she asked herself, "if my small feet can climb so high?"

Slowly, she began to make her way upward. Suddenly, the ground grew dark around her. The earth shook as something landed close by. It was Shadow of the Air!

"Have you lost your way?" He asked. "I do not often see the Small Eyes of the Little Feet when I hunt each day on the Great Mountain."

Little One had never seen Shadow of the Air up close. His great eyes and sharp beak frightened her, but she did not run away.

"The Maker of Life is sending me on a journey to the Land of the Tamer of Beasts," she said. "I have traveled through the Land of the Deep Grass, and now I must cross the Great Mountain that Touches the Sky."

Shadow of the Air thought for a moment. "Why is the Maker of Life sending you on such a long and difficult journey?" he asked.

"I do not know why," Little One answered.

"Well," he said, "it seems silly to me to do something and not know why."

"I do not have to know why," she said. "It is enough that the Maker of Life knows why."

Shadow of the Air looked into her trusting eyes. "I will help the Maker of Life," he said. "Do not be afraid. We will cross the Great Mountain together."

Gently he picked her up and lifted her into the air. As he beat his mighty wings, Little One was carried over the Great Mountain. As Shadow of the Air set her down, she could see in the distance the Land of the Great Forest.

Your love, O Lord, reaches to the heavens, your faithfulness to the skies.

Psalm 36:5

Little One began to cross the Land of the Great Forest. Soon she became very tired, and she knew she must find a place to rest. She made her way to an open space beside a fallen log and sat down. She had not been there long when she heard a deep voice behind her.

"What do you think you are doing," it said, "sitting in my resting place?"

Little One turned, and there before her was Roar of the Long Teeth! She could feel his hot breath upon her face, but she did not run away.

"I am sorry if this is your resting place," she said. "The Maker of Life is sending me on a journey to the Land of the Tamer of Beasts. I have already crossed the Land of the Deep Grass and the Great Mountain that Touches the Sky. But the Land of the Great Forest is not easy for me to walk through."

Roar of the Long Teeth thought for a moment. "I am one of the strongest of beasts," he said. "But it would be very hard for even me to cross the Land of the Great Forest. How do you, the weakest of beasts, expect to make such a journey?"

"My strength comes from the Maker of Life," Little One answered.

Roar of the Long Teeth looked into her trusting eyes. "I will help the Maker of Life," he said. "We will cross the Land of the Great Forest together."

He lowered his head, and Little One climbed up to the thick fur that lay between his great ears.

As Roar of the Long Teeth carried her along, she was thankful to be riding such a powerful beast. It was not until the next morning that he made his way out of the forest. He helped her down. She thanked him and then scampered away through the rocks and small tufts of grass that covered the ground.

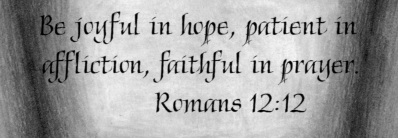

Be joyful in hope, patient in affliction, faithful in prayer.

Romans 12:12

Little One continued on her way. "I wonder how far the Water of the Deep Bottom can be," she thought. She had not gone far when she stopped to sniff the air. Something was coming, and it was not an animal. It was Fingers of Death, and its dark breath was all around her!

As she moved along, it became hard to breathe, and she found it difficult to see the way before her. Soon she could go no farther. Then in a soft voice she said,

"Maker of Life, I am such a small creature, and I know you have much to do taking care of all that lives upon the earth. But I am afraid, and I need your help. I know that you love me, and I thank you for watching over me. Please show me the way I must go."

It was not long before she saw two feet of great size beside her. It was Mountain that Walks! Slowly he lifted her above the dark breath that had frightened her so.

"You are very kind," she said. "Thank you for helping me."

Mountain that Walks thought for a moment. Then he said, "You are such a small creature to be traveling all alone. Where are you going?"

"The Maker of Life," said Little One, "is sending me on a journey to the Land of the Tamer of Beasts. I have already crossed the Land of the Deep Grass, the Great Mountain that Touches the Sky, and the Land of the Great Forest. I am now on my way to the Water of the Deep Bottom."

Mountain that Walks looked into her trusting eyes. "I will help the Maker of Life," he said. He held her gently and turned away from the path where Fingers of Death would soon be coming. He quickly carried her to a place where she would be safe. He helped her to the ground and she hurried on her way.

O Lord God Almighty, who is like you? You are mighty, O Lord, and your faithfulness surrounds you.

Psalm 89:8

It was not long before Little One found herself standing before the Water of the Deep Bottom.

"It is too wide for me to swim," she thought. "Perhaps I can float across." And she climbed upon a log that was moving slowly in the water.

She had not traveled far when she heard a strange voice. "Pardon me," it said, "but how can I see where I am going if you are sitting in front of my eyes?"

Little One looked behind her. "Please forgive me," she said, "but I have never seen a talking log with eyes before."

"I am not a log," said the voice. "I am Eyes Above the Water."

Little One looked closely. She could see his broad back and long tail. She had heard of Eyes Above the Water. Even the greatest of beasts feared his powerful jaws. She was afraid, but she did not swim away.

"The Maker of Life is sending me on a journey to the Land of the Tamer of Beasts," she said.

Eyes Above the Water thought for a moment. "I have heard," he said, "that something very strange is happening in the Land of the Tamer of Beasts. You may find danger there."

"The Maker of Life," Little One replied, "has guided me through the Land of the Deep Grass, over the Great Mountain that Touches the Sky, and across the Land of the Great Forest. He has saved me from Fingers of Death. I know he will protect me from danger in the Land of the Tamer of Beasts."

Eyes Above the Water looked into her trusting eyes. "I will help the Maker of Life," he said. "The Land of the Tamer of Beasts is close by."

Slowly he began to swim across the Water of the Deep Bottom. When he reached the other side, he crawled up the bank and set her on dry land.

You are to bring into the ark
two of all living creatures,
male and female, to keep
them alive with you... Noah
did everything just as God
commanded him.

Genesis 6:19, 22

Little One was very tired. "I have come such a long way," she said to herself. "I hope the Land of the Tamer of Beasts is not too far."

As she walked along, the air was filled with the sounds of many feet walking upon the earth. She walked faster. The sounds grew closer. Suddenly she saw them. Young beasts of all kinds were making their way to a great shadow that rose high above the ground.

"What can this be?" she asked herself aloud.

"It is called an ark," said a voice behind her. "It was built by one of the Tamers of Beasts. His name is Noah, and the Maker of Life has placed us in his care."

Little One turned, and standing before her was one of her own kind. "How do you know this?" she asked.

"The Maker of Life," he answered, "made this known to me as I journeyed to this land. I know that you are called Little One and you have come from a far place. It is the wish of the Maker of Life that we join the other beasts and enter the ark."

Little One thought for a moment. "What will happen when we go inside?" she asked.

"This I do not know," he answered. "But I do know that each beast that enters the ark will be blessed by the Maker of Life."

Little One looked into his trusting eyes. "Then let us go together," she said.

She went to his side, and they made their way to the ark, where they would find a new life together.

To order additional copies of

Little One

Have your credit card ready and call

Toll free: (877) 421-READ (7323)

or order online at: www.winepressbooks.com